GALAXY ZACK

A GREEN CHRISTMAS!

By Ray O'Ryan

Illustrated by Colin Jack

LITTLE SIMON

New York   London   Toronto   Sydney   New Delhi

This book is a work of fiction. Any references to historical events, real people, or real places are used fictitiously. Other names, characters, places, and events are products of the author's imagination, and any resemblance to actual events or places or persons, living or dead, is entirely coincidental.

LITTLE SIMON

An imprint of Simon & Schuster
Children's Publishing Division
1230 Avenue of the Americas,
New York, New York 10020
Copyright © 2013 by Simon & Schuster, Inc.
All rights reserved, including the right of
reproduction in whole or in part in any form.
LITTLE SIMON is a registered trademark
of Simon & Schuster, Inc., and associated
colophon is a trademark of
Simon & Schuster, Inc.
For information about special discounts
for bulk purchases, please contact
Simon & Schuster Special Sales
at 1-866-506-1949 or
business@simonandschuster.com.
The Simon & Schuster Speakers
Bureau can bring authors to your live
event. For more information or to book
an event contact the Simon & Schuster
Speakers Bureau at 1-866-248-3049 or
visit our website at
www.simonspeakers.com.
Initial interior sketches by Andrew Murray
Designed by Ciara Gay
Manufactured in the United States of America
0813 FFG
First Edition 1 2 3 4 5 6 7 8 9 10
Library of Congress
Cataloging-in-Publication Data
O'Ryan, Ray.
A green Christmas! / by Ray O'Ryan ;
illustrated by Colin Jack. — 1st edition.
p. cm. — (Galaxy Zack ; 6)
Summary: When a cosmic storm hits, stranding the Nelsons on their new home
planet, Nebulon, Zack's hopes of a white Christmas in Vermont are dashed, but
Nebulon provides a surprising alternative.
ISBN 978-1-4424-8224-1 (pbk. : alk. paper)
ISBN 978-1-4424-8225-8 (hardcover : alk. paper)
ISBN 978-1-4424-8226-5 (ebook : alk. paper)
[1. Science fiction. 2. Snow — Fiction. 3. Christmas — Fiction.
4. Outer space — Fiction.] I. Jack, Colin, illustrator. II. Title.
PZ7.O7843Gre 2013
[Fic] — dc23
2012045337

CONTENTS

Chapter 1

Holiday Plans

Zack Nelson stretched out on his bed with his dog, Luna, beside him. He clutched his hyperphone and punched in the z-mail address for his cousin Louis on Earth. Christmas was coming, and Zack was already on his school break.

Zack was born on Earth. He had spent the first eight years of his life living in Dubbsville, Texas. But Zack now lived on the planet Nebulon.

Zack and his family had moved to Nebulon several months ago. At first Zack missed Earth very much and he

wished he could go back and live there
again. But Zack had grown to really
like his life on Nebulon, even though
he still missed his friends and family
on Earth.

As Zack's hyperphone blazed to
life, his cousin Louis's face appeared

on the screen.

"Begin video chat," said a computer voice from the device.

"Hey, Zack! How's life on Nebulon?" asked Louis.

"Pretty good," replied Zack, "but I can't wait to get back to Earth for Christmas!"

This would be Zack's first Christmas since his family moved to Nebulon. But Zack, his mom and dad, and his twin sisters, Charlotte and Cathy, were planning on traveling back to Earth. Zack loved spending Christmas with his relatives. Louis and his family lived in Vermont, and Zack always looked forward to sledding and building snowmen with his cousins.

"We already have about eight inches of snow here," said Louis, "and they are expecting more by Christmas!"

"Yippee wah-wah!" Zack shouted.

"Yippee what?" asked Louis.

"Oh, that's just something we say here on Nebulon when we're really happy about something," Zack explained, "and I'm SO excited about playing in all that snow with you!"

"Me too!" said Louis. "Does it ever snow on Nebulon?"

"No," said Zack. "It gets cold, but not cold enough to snow. That's why I'm so glad I'm coming to Earth! It just wouldn't feel like Christmas without snow."

"And without you!" Louis added.

"Yeah!" Zack cried.

7

"Do they have Christmas on Nebulon?" Louis asked.

"Yeah," said Zack, "but from what I've seen so far, it's really different. The Christmas trees look weird. So do the ornaments. The trees look like long tubes of light. The ornaments are all square-looking and metal. I guess they're okay, but I prefer the ones that we have on Earth."

Just then Louis held his hyperphone up to his bedroom window. "Look!" he said.

8

Zack saw what was happening outside: White snow was falling gently on the Vermont mountains.

"Wow!" said Zack. "It's beautiful. This is going to be the best Christmas ever!"

Ruff! Ruff! Luna barked excitedly.

Chapter 2

Shopping Time!

The next morning Zack hurried into the kitchen. His parents and his sisters were already having breakfast.

"Good morning, Master Just Zack," said Ira. "What would you like to eat this morning?"

Ira was the Nelson family's Indoor

Robotic Assistant. Although Ira was a machine, he had a personality. Zack had come to think of Ira as part of the family.

"I'd like a couple of eggs, cosmic-style, and toast with boingoberry jam, please," replied Zack.

"Guess where . . ."

". . . we're going . . ."

". . . today?" asked Charlotte and Cathy.

The twins always finished each other's sentences.

Zack looked at his mom and dad.

"We're going on a shopping trip to the planet Cisnos," Mom explained.

"Cisnos?" said Zack. "That's the planet with the really grape Lollyland amusement park. I love that place."

"Same planet, Captain," said Dad, using his favorite nickname for Zack. "Only instead of going to the amusement park, we'll be going to the mall. It's holiday shopping time!"

"And it's not just any mall . . ."

". . . it's the Cisnos Mondo-Mall . . ."

". . . the biggest mall in this part

of the galaxy!" Charlotte and Cathy squealed with delight. They both loved to go shopping.

"Your father and I figured that we would do all our shopping before our trip to Earth," Mom explained. "That way when we get to Earth, we can start celebrating right away!"

"Ugh," Zack moaned. "I'd rather go to the amusement park."

"They've got the biggest food court in the entire sector . . . ," Dad pointed out.

Zack's eyes opened wide. "What time do we leave?" he asked, smiling.

Just then a panel in the kitchen wall

slid out. Out came a mechanical arm holding a plate of steaming eggs and toast.

"Here is your breakfast, Master Just Zack," said Ira.

"We leave just as soon as you finish eating," Mom said.

"Grape!" said Zack. He shoved a

forkful of eggs into his mouth.

Zack was looking forward to seeing what the Christmas decorations on Cisnos looked like. But he still couldn't wait to get back to Earth to celebrate the old fashioned way.

19

Chapter 3

Off to Cisnos!

The Nelson family piled into their car. They took off for the Creston City Spaceport where they would catch the shuttle to Cisnos. Zack had been to the Creston City Spaceport many times. He loved space travel.

The Nelsons soon arrived. Once

everyone got out of the car, Dad pressed a button on the hood. The tires folded up into the bumpers and the trunk slipped underneath. A few seconds later the car had turned into a small green square.

Dad picked up the green square. It was very light. He slipped it into a storage slot.

"The Nebulon version of a parking garage!" said Dad.

"I love that!" said Zack.

"Me too," said Dad.

"The Cisnos Shuttle is now boarding

at Landing Pod seventy-seven," said an announcement over the spaceport's loudspeakers.

"Here we go!" said Dad.

The Nelsons boarded the shuttle. A few minutes later they were zooming through space.

Zack stared out the shuttle window. Nebulon grew smaller and smaller.

"What are you going to look for at the mall, girls?" Mom asked

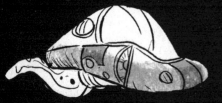

Charlotte and Cathy.

"We want to get that new doll . . ."

". . . Orbiting Alice . . ."

". . . the doll that flies around the room . . ."

". . . as a gift . . ."

". . . for cousin Susie in Vermont," the twins replied.

"Very nice," said Mom. "How about you, Zack?"

"I don't know," said Zack. "I was thinking about getting Louis a book

about galactic blast. I know how much he likes baseball. I thought he might like to read about the version we play here on Nebulon."

"All of you have such good ideas," said Mom.

Zack stared out the window and watched stars zip through space. But all he could think about at that moment was playing in the snow back on Earth.

A short while later, an orange planet came into view.

"There it is!" cried Zack. "Cisnos!"

"Wow . . ."

". . . pretty!" said Charlotte and Cathy.

As the shuttle dropped through purple clouds, a huge shopping mall appeared below. The mall was ten times bigger than any mall Zack had ever seen on Earth!

After the shuttle landed, Zack followed his family and stepped onto a moving sidewalk. The sidewalk led

VID ZONE

them right into the mall.

Stores were everywhere. Zack looked up and saw that the mall spread out in every direction.

"How do we even know where to begin?" he asked.

Chapter 4

Mall Madness!

"Welcome, Nelson family," said a woman's voice right above Zack's head. "What are you looking for?"

Zack jumped. He was startled by this unexpected voice. Looking up, he saw a small round metal ball hovering in the air.

"I am Midge—your Mall Interactive Directory Guide Escort," said a voice coming from a speaker on the flying ball. "I am here to help you."

"This thing reminds me of Ira," Zack said.

"Correct," said Midge. "The Indoor Robotic Assistant was developed in the same lab as I was."

"We want . . ."

". . . to find . . ."

". . . dolls!" squealed Charlotte and Cathy.

"Certainly," said Midge.

Suddenly, Charlotte and Cathy saw their names appear, flashing along the floor in front of them.

"Simply follow your names," said Midge.

"I wanna go to the food court!" said Zack.

"Certainly," said Midge.

Zack's name appeared right at his feet.

"I will keep track of all family

members," explained Midge. "I will make sure you do not get lost and that you will find each other later."

"Grape!" said Zack. He started following his name as it moved along the floor. "See ya later!" Zack called out to his family.

"Okay," said Mom, a bit concerned.

"Be careful, Zack. You too, girls!"

"Do not worry," said Midge. "I will keep an eye on them."

Zack followed his name along the floor. Every store he passed was filled with Christmas decorations. But the decorations Zack saw didn't look like the ones he knew from Earth.

Instead of Christmas trees, the Cisnosians and the Nebulites used thin glowing tubes. The tubes were shaped to look like tree branches. Zack thought they looked unfriendly. He loved the look and smell of the real evergreen Christmas trees that grew on Earth.

Ornaments hung from the glowing tubes—but they were different, too. These ornaments had sharp angles. Zack preferred the homemade ornaments his family used each year. They always gave him a warm, cozy feeling.

I'm glad we're going to Earth for Christmas, thought Zack. *Here they have no snow, no real Christmas trees, and weird-looking ornaments.*

"You have arrived at the food court," said Midge, who reappeared.

The voice startled Zack. He had been busy following his name and looking in all the store windows. He had forgotten all about Midge.

"Thanks, Midge," Zack said. Then he ran into the food court.

Zack bought a bag of fritter loops and began munching. They reminded him of the curly fries he used to get on Earth. Next he gobbled up a galactic stack, the biggest sandwich on Cisnos. Then he washed it all down with a swirlie—a really delicious,

sweet, fruity frozen drink.
*The food at this mall sure
is good!* Zack thought.

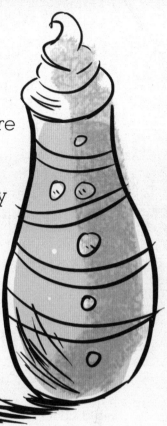

He suddenly
remembered that he
had to buy Louis's
present. "Midge,
can you lead me
to a bookstore?"
Zack asked.

"Certainly," replied Midge.
"Just follow your name."

Once again, Zack's name
appeared at his feet. He
followed his name to a store

called the Universe of Books. Inside,
Zack saw tall stacks of books of every
size and shape.

Zack stepped up to a small view
screen. "Books about sports, please,"
he said.

The view screen blazed to life, and

a series of arrows showed a path through the store. Zack followed the arrows and arrived at a whole shelf of books about galactic blast.

Zack looked through several books until he found just the right one. "This one's perfect!" he said, grabbing a big book off the shelf. "*The History of Galactic Blast.* I bet Louis is going to love it!"

After Zack bought the book, he stepped out of the store. But as he turned, he found himself face to face with Seth Stevens, the biggest bully in his class!

45

Chapter 5
A Storm Is Brewing

"Hi, Seth," said Zack.

When Zack first arrived at the Sprockets Academy, Seth bullied him. But over time, the two started to get along.

"Hi, Zack. What did you get?" Seth asked.

"It's a book about galactic blast for my cousin," Zack explained. "We're going back to Earth for Christmas."

"That sounds like fun," said Seth.

"What's that?" Zack asked, pointing.

Seth was holding something hard and plastic. It looked like a shiny boot.

"It is my Christmas stocking, of course," Seth replied. "Have you not seen one before?"

"Sure," said Zack. "But the ones we use on Earth are soft and made from cloth."

"Weird," said Seth. Then he walked

 away, shaking his head.

"Excuse me, but it is time for you to rejoin your parents," said Midge. She had been hovering nearby, out of sight. "I will show you the way."

Once again, Zack's name lit up on the floor. He followed a series of purple lights, which led to the bottom of a really long escalator. The rest of Zack's family was waiting there.

"How did you do?" Mom asked.

"I got Louis this book," Zack said, holding up the book about galactic blast.

"We got . . ."

". . . Orbiting Alice. Look . . ."

". . . she flies!" said Charlotte and Cathy.

The twins pulled a doll out of the bag they were holding. She wore a shiny uniform and had a helmet on her head. When Cathy pressed a button on the doll's back, Orbiting Alice took off. She zoomed into the air and reached the top of the escalator. Then she flew right back into Cathy's hands.

"Pretty cool . . . for a doll," admitted Zack.

Zack noticed that his mom and dad had lots of big bags.

"What did you and Dad get?" he asked Mom.

"Never mind!" replied Mom, smiling. "You'll find out on Christmas Day!"

"Okay, gang," said Dad. "Let's all

head up to the shuttle."

The Nelsons stepped onto the escalator. As they traveled up, they passed a series of huge screens. Each screen floated in the air. One screen showed a reporter covering a news story. The next one had the sports report. But it was the last screen that caught Zack's eye. Maps, graphs, and images of the planet Cisnos filled the screen. A Cisnosian weather reporter spoke. "It appears that a huge cosmic storm is

headed right for us."

A scary image then filled the screen. A huge blue-and-yellow swirling storm moved through space. In the bottom corner of the screen, Cisnos looked like a tiny marble. The storm spun right toward the planet.

"Hmm . . . ," said Dad as they reached the top of the escalator. "That is one *big* storm. And if a storm that big hits Cisnos, it's going to affect us on Nebulon, too."

"What does that mean, Dad?" asked Zack.

"I'm not sure yet," Dad replied. "We'll just have to wait and see."

The Nelsons reached the shuttle and settled into their seats. Soon the shuttle took off, whisking them back to Nebulon.

Zack had an uneasy feeling in his stomach the whole ride home.

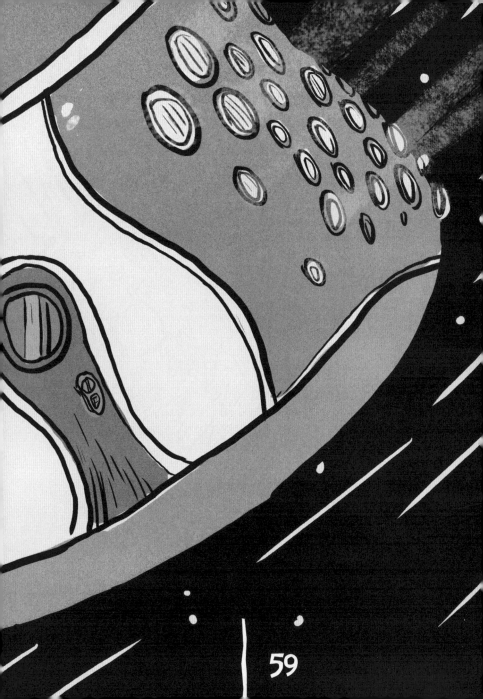

Chapter 6

Time for Christmas!

When the Nelsons got home, Zack flipped on the sonic cell monitor, which looked like a giant TV screen. Soon one wall of the living room blazed to life.

On the screen, Zack saw images of the same storm he had seen at the mall. Luna sat beside him.

"All the weather experts agree," said the reporter on the screen. "Nebulon has never seen a storm like this before."

The sonic cell monitor showed the giant storm. Streaks of blue and yellow spun around each other. The storm kept changing shape.

Nebulon appeared on the screen.

"Wow!" exclaimed Zack. "Nebulon looks super-small next to that gigantic cosmic storm."

"Daddy, what will happen . . ."

". . . when the storm . . ."

". . . comes here?" asked Charlotte and Cathy.

"That's exactly what I'm going to find out," said Dad. "I'm heading to Nebulonics. We can study this storm."

"Don't be too long," Mom said.

After Dad left, Zack looked up at

63

his mom. He was starting to feel a little scared. He saw that his sisters were nervous too.

"How about we forget about the storm for a while?" asked Mom. "Let's decorate the house for Christmas!"

"Sure!" said Zack. In all the excitement about the storm, he had almost forgotten about Christmas!

"Ira, Christmas boxes, please," said Mom.

"Certainly, Mrs. Nelson," replied Ira.

A small door in the living room opened. Then several boxes slid out. Each of the boxes was labeled with what was inside.

"I haven't seen these boxes since I packed them up on Earth," Mom said.

Zack and his sisters helped Mom open and empty the boxes. Out came all their favorite ornaments and decorations.

"Here's our indoor tree!" exclaimed Zack. On Earth, the Nelsons always had a real Christmas tree outside, and a plastic one inside.

Zack pulled out three sections of a big green plastic tree. Mom helped him snap the pieces together. When they finished, a big Christmas tree stood tall in the living room.

"Now it . . ."

". . . looks like . . ."

"Christmas!" the twins squealed
with delight.

"Hey, I found our stockings!" yelled Zack.

He pulled six cloth stockings out of a box. Each one was trimmed with a gold ribbon and had a name stitched across the front. Every member of the family—including Luna—had one.

"Charlotte, here's your stocking," Zack said, handing it to his sister. "And Cathy, here's yours."

Luna barked happily and wagged her tail.

Zack knelt down and showed Luna her stocking. "And

look, Luna!" he exclaimed. "This is your stocking. I'll bet there will be a new chew toy in there this year!"

Luna barked again.

Zack looked at his own stocking. He thought about past Christmases.

"But, Mom, where are we going to hang them?" Zack asked. "We don't have a fireplace here like we did on Earth. Here, Ira keeps the house warm."

"Excuse me,

but I believe I can help," said Ira.

A panel slid open in the floor and a fireplace mantel rose into the room.

"Thank you, Ira," said Mom.

"That's amazing, Ira!" cried Zack. "It looks just like our old mantel back on Earth."

"I used the family photos you downloaded into my system as a

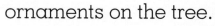

reference guide," Ira explained.

Zack and his sisters hung all the stockings on the mantel.

Next came the tree decorating. Zack and his sisters placed their favorite ornaments on the tree.

Cathy hung a tiny silver angel on the highest branch

she could reach. "This is the first
ornament I ever got."

"Here's my favorite," said Zack.
He placed an ornament shaped like
a rocket ship on the tree.
"Time for liftoff, Captain."

Just then everyone
heard Dad's car land

in the garage. Zack could tell that something was wrong as soon as Dad rushed into the living room.

"Bad news, gang," said Dad. "Our equipment at the office showed that the storm is definitely going to hit Nebulon. It's not safe to travel."

"On no!" said Mom.

"What?" cried Zack.

"I'm sorry," said Dad. "But we have to cancel our trip to Earth."

Chapter 7

A Change of Plans

"I can't believe we won't be going to Earth for Christmas!" Zack said.

"I know, honey," said Mom. "We're all disappointed."

"We really don't know what to expect with this storm," explained Dad. "No one is sure what will happen here on

Nebulon, but we *do* know it will make space travel unsafe."

Dad stepped back outside. A moment later he returned with a tall box.

"Since we are going to be spending Christmas on Nebulon, I thought I'd get a few of their traditional decorations," he said.

Dad opened the box and pulled out a series

of glowing neon tubes. When he
put them all together, they formed a
Nebulon Christmas tree.

"That's weird," said Zack.

"It *is* kind of different," Mom

admitted. "But it's nice to experience how the holiday is celebrated in our new home."

"I also got these," Dad said. He opened a square box filled with Nebulon Christmas ornaments.

Zack pulled a small ornament out of the box. It was a shiny piece of metal in a zigzag shape. He hung it on the neon tree.

"Weird," he said. "But kinda cool, I guess."

"Look at . . ."

". . . this crazy . . ."

". . . ornament," said the twins.

Cathy held up a round ornament. It had a tiny video screen on it that showed a bunch of flashing lights.

Cathy hung the ornament on the neon tree.

"Excuse me, but Master Drake is at the door," Ira said suddenly.

"Drake's here," said Zack. "Grape!"

Drake Taylor was Zack's best friend on Nebulon.

"Hi, everyone," said Drake.

"Hello, Drake," Mom said. "Nice to see you."

"Did you hear about the big storm heading right for Nebulon?" Drake asked.

"Sure did," said Dad.

"Yeah, we had to cancel our trip back to Earth," said Zack.

"Too bad," said Drake. "I know you were looking forward to it."

"Christmas on Earth is really great," said Zack. "Every year we would go to my cousin's house in Vermont. We always had a white Christmas."

"What is a white Christmas?" asked Drake.

"The snow makes everything white," Zack explained.

"Oh, I have heard of snow," said Drake. "I saw pictures in a sonic cell vid once. It looks pretty, but cold."

"You're right—it *is* cold," said Zack.

"But once you are out playing in it, you don't even feel the cold. You build snowmen. You go sledding. It's really grape!"

"So Christmas on Earth is pretty different, huh?" asked Drake.

"You bet!" Zack replied. "Even the trees are different. Every year we would decorate our tree with ornaments we made ourselves. We hung strings of popcorn. We put on bright, flashing lights. And we placed a gold star at the very top."

"Speaking of homemade ornaments," interrupted Mom, "look what I found!"

Chapter 8
Christmas Memories

Mom put an old box on the table.

"These are the first ornaments you ever made, Zack," Mom said. "I think you were in kindergarten."

Mom pulled out an ornament made from uncooked elbow macaroni. Zack had glued the pieces of macaroni together to form a robot.

"I remember that one!" said Zack.

Mom also took out a paper snowflake from the box. It had been cut out and sprinkled with glitter. She hung both ornaments on the green Christmas tree the Nelsons had brought from Earth.

"Wow!" exclaimed Drake. "Those are really nice,

Zack. On Nebulon nobody makes homemade ornaments. We buy all of ours."

"It's fun to make your own ornaments," said Zack. "Then it's fun to see them again each year when you hang them on the tree."

"On Earth, the memories of past Christmases make each new holiday that much more special," explained Mom.

"Look, Mom . . ."

". . . here are the fuzzy reindeer ornaments that . . ."

". . . we made last year!" said the twins.

Cathy and Charlotte hung their felt reindeer ornaments on the tree.

"What is a reindeer?" asked Drake.

"It's an animal on Earth," explained Zack. "Flying reindeer pull Santa's sleigh so he can deliver presents to kids all around the world."

"Oh,"
said Drake.
"Santa brings us presents too. But on Nebulon, he flies an atomic-powered jet sleigh."

"I don't mean to rush you, Drake," said Dad, "but the storm could hit at any time now. I want you to be safe at home with your family before it strikes."

"Thanks, Mr. Nelson," said Drake. Then he jumped back on his bike and headed for home.

How bad will this storm be? Zack wondered. *I hope everyone will be all right.*

Chapter 9

The Cosmic Storm

Zack had trouble sleeping that night. Every few minutes he jumped out of bed and ran to the window. He kept checking to see if the storm had begun.

He finally dozed off.

When Zack woke up in the morning, the sky was filled with dark gray clouds.

He joined his family at the kitchen table.

"It's kinda scary-looking out there," said Zack.

"I was just watching the sonic cell," said Dad. "They expect the storm to hit at any moment."

After breakfast the Nelsons gathered in their living room. Mom and Dad sat on the couch. Cathy and Charlotte curled up in their cozy blankets on the rug. Zack sat in his

favorite chair. Luna stretched out on the floor.

Suddenly the room got very dark. Zack looked out the big living room window. The sky had turned from gray to solid black. It looked more like midnight than morning. The whistling noise changed to a screech as the wind picked up. Zack saw the tall trees in front of the house shake and sway back and forth.

"It's starting," Zack said softly.

The house began to shake. Windows rattled. Pictures on the wall swung back and forth.

A wind-blown tree scraped against the side of the house. Luna yelped and jumped up into Zack's lap.

"It's okay, Luna," said Zack, scratching her head. "It's just a little wind."

But Zack was getting scared too.

A few minutes later the wind died down. Things got weirdly quiet. Zack ran to the living room window and could not believe what he was seeing.

"Dad—look!" he called. His mouth hung open in wonder.

Tiny green flakes were falling from the sky.

"I'm going out!" said Dad, grabbing his Nebulonics suit. "Wait here."

Zack watched through the window. The falling green flakes seemed to get bigger. Soon a curtain of green was falling from the sky. As they fell,

the flakes stuck to the ground!

Dad put out his hand. A few green flakes hit his glove . . . and melted! Dad hurried back into the house.

"It's snow!" cried Zack. "Green snow! We're going to have snow at Christmas, after all! We can sled and build green snowmen and—"

"Slow down a second, Zack," said Dad. "I know it looks like green snow. But before I let anyone play in it, I need to know exactly what it is."

At that moment Dad's hyperphone began buzzing.

"Otto Nelson," he said flipping the device open. "Yes, I'll be right there."

Dad put his hyperphone away and headed for the garage.

"That was Fred Stevens from Nebulonics," Dad explained. "He's calling the whole team together. No one has ever seen anything like this. We've got to figure out exactly what this green stuff is!"

Chapter 10

A Green Christmas!

Zack paced back and forth in front of the living room window. Charlotte and Cathy followed his every step. Every minute seemed to take an hour.

"What's taking Dad so long?" he asked impatiently.

"Honey, you heard your father,"

Mom said. "No one knows what this green stuff is. They need to figure out whether or not it's safe."

Zack watched as the green flakes began to pile higher and higher. He could hardly see the street anymore. Everything was green!

Zack thought about all the great times he had playing with his cousins in Vermont. Christmas and snow just went together.

He thought about the canceled trip

to Earth. Now he waited to see if there'd be snow in his Christmas after all.

Zack flipped on the sonic cell monitor. Every channel showed pictures of the mysterious green flakes piling up. Nervous Nebulites stared out their windows.

An hour passed. Zack could hardly stand the wait.

"Mr. Nelson has returned," Ira announced finally.

Dad walked into the living room. He shook green flakes from his coat.

"Well, what are you guys sitting around for?" he asked. "Don't you want to go out and play in the snow?"

"It's safe?" Mom asked cautiously.

"Yup," Dad replied. "We ran a full analysis. We're not exactly sure why it's green, but it's probably because of the storm. It is definitely snow though.

First time ever on Nebulon. And it is definitely safe!"

"Yay!" Zack and the twins all shouted together.

Everyone bundled up. Dad took some old boxes and metal railings

and helped the kids build some sleds.

Zack, his sisters, and Luna walked up to the highest point in their yard. They climbed onto their sleds and took turns zooming down the hill

"Wheee!" cried Zack. "This is totally grape!"

A few minutes later, Drake and his

parents showed up.

"I just heard on the sonic cell that this green stuff is safe," Drake said.

"I told you about snow," Zack said. "And now you get to play in it!"

Drake's mom and dad watched as he climbed onto the sled with Zack. Both boys raced down the hill. They toppled

into the snow and laughed.

One by one, curious Nebulites came out. They were amazed at seeing snow for the very first time.

Some Nebulites began building snowmen. Others flopped down and made green snow angels. Snowballs flew softly through the air as squeals of delight could be heard from kids and adults alike.

"You know, Drake," Zack said as they got ready for another ride. "A white Christmas would have been fun. But a green Christmas is the best!"

GALAXY ZACK

ADVENTURE!

HERE'S A SNEAK PEEK!

"Good morning, everyone," Drake said. "Thank you for inviting me on this trip."

"We're glad you could make it," replied Mom.

"Okay—I'm ready!" Zack said, tossing his napkin onto his empty plate.

and jumping from his seat. "Let's go!"

"What about . . ."

". . . Luna?"

"Can she come?" asked the twins.

"It wouldn't be a family trip without Luna!" said Dad. "Come on, girl!"

Everyone piled into the family's flying car and headed to the Creston City Spaceport. A short while later they climbed into a shuttle and took off.

Zack smiled as stars and planets whizzed past him. Space travel always made him happy. Zack and Drake played games with their hyperphones until . . .

"Look . . ."

". . . there it is . . ."

". . . Gluco!" cried the girls, pointing out the window.

Zack peered out the shuttle's window. Below he saw a bright blue planet that was shaped like a giant jelly bean in space.

As the shuttle dropped down for its landing, it passed through what looked like a layer of clouds.

"These clouds are made of cotton candy!" said Drake.

"This is going to be great!" cried Zack.

An excerpt from *A Galactic Easter!*